How to Tame a Bully

by
Nancy Wilcox Richards

ILLUSTRATED BY
Drazen Kozjan

Scholastic Inc.

New York Toronto London Auckland
Sydney Mexico City New Delhi Hong Kong

ISBN-13: 978-0-545-20909-0
ISBN-10 0-545-20909-9

12 11 10 9 8 7 6 5 4 3   9 10 11 12 13 14/0

Printed in the U.S.A.
First American edition, October 2009

For Nicholas, who battles the biggest bully, leukemia;

and for my three other nephews:

James, Aaron, and Matthew.

— N.W.R.

Chapter 1

My name is Lauren — Lauren Campbell. This year I'm going into third grade and I know, just know, it's going to be my best year ever.

First of all, I've got Ms. MacArthur. She's the teacher everyone wants. No homework on the weekends, free time every Friday afternoon, and she has a jelly-bean machine right in the classroom. Sometimes if you do your homework you get money for the machine.

I was so excited on the first day of school when I saw my name on the list outside her room. I had really lucked out! Then I saw the name of my best friend, Claire. Bonus!

I walked in and took the seat closest to

the computers. I didn't check to see who else was at my table. I just wanted to be near the computers. That way when I finished my work, I'd have a pretty good chance of getting to use them first. No racing from one end of the room to the other, which would mean being sent back to my seat for running.

What I didn't figure on was sitting next to Bethany — the biggest bully at Bayfield Elementary. But when I turned around, there she was, sitting right beside me — Bayfield's very own, very mean Bethany Walters.

Bethany is a giant. She is almost as tall as Ms. MacArthur. And that's when she's sitting down. Her arms are really long. Maybe they got stretched from reaching out and grabbing kids — before she choked them. Her eyes are always moving. Watching everyone. I know what she's doing. She's looking for her next victim. Someone she can force to do her homework. Someone she can beat up. Well, it isn't going to be me. I'm out of here. Computer or no computer — it just isn't worth it.

I knew I had to change seats, and fast. But before I could pick up my bookbag and move, Ms. MacArthur said, "Why, Lauren! I'm so glad you decided to sit at this table. I'm sure you and Bethany will become good friends as the year goes on."

I smiled weakly back at the teacher. "Sure," I mumbled, not really meaning it.

"You know, Lauren, Bethany only moved to Bayfield last spring," continued Ms. MacArthur. "This is a chance for her to meet lots more kids." She smiled at Bethany. "I hope you have a wonderful year with us."

I wanted to say, "What about *my* year? What about *me*?" but instead I glanced over at Bethany. She glared at me. Her beady little eyes squinted. She reminded me of a cornered rat. Slowly she raised a hand and folded her fingers down one at a time until she had made a fist. A knuckle sandwich. I got the message real fast. Bethany and I were never going to be friends. Not now. Not next year. Not ever. N-E-V-E-R.

Third grade had just gotten off to a terrible start.

Chapter 2

"Why did you sit with Bethany?" Claire asked me at recess. "You want to die or something? She's crazy!"

"Yeah." I nodded glumly. "I didn't plan it that way. I didn't see her sitting at the table. All I was thinking about was being near the computers."

Claire gave me a look of sympathy. "Too late now," she said. "You know what? This is her second year in third grade. She's really supposed to be in fourth grade. And she's big enough for fifth grade."

I nodded again.

"And guess what. Last year she took Kirsten Whynot's tooth that the dentist had pulled and put it under *her own* pillow. The tooth fairy didn't come, of course. And I heard she gave Kris Vaughan such a wedgie that his underwear was pulled up to his chin!" Claire took a big breath and continued, "*And* she made Aaron Frielink eat worms from Mr. Blair's science room."

I groaned out loud. This was worse than I had imagined! I could see it now — my mother and father crying at my funeral, wondering how things could ever have gone so wrong.

Just then Claire said, "Don't look now, but Bethany looks really mad and she's heading our way."

I glanced over my shoulder and sure enough, Claire was right. Bethany was marching across the playground. She was headed straight for me.

"Hey, Shrimp!" she yelled.

I looked back toward the swing set. I mean, I know I'm the second-shortest kid in third grade, but maybe, just maybe she was hollering at someone else. No such luck. The

swing set was empty. I turned and faced
Bethany. "Me?" I squeaked out.

"Yeah, you. Who else would I be talking
to, Shrimp?"

I swallowed. "What do you want?"

"Your snack, to start with," said Bethany. "And from now on, you better make sure you bring me a recess snack every day. You got that?" Then she grabbed the brownie right out of my hand and stuffed it into her mouth. Her cheeks bulged out and her lips puckered as she gobbled it down. She reminded me of a chipmunk with its pouches full of nuts. One bite and my mom's famous double-fudge chocolate brownie was gone.

Bethany wiped her sleeve across her face, cleaning off the leftover chocolate smears. "Not bad, Shrimp. Not bad. Remember to bring more tomorrow, or else!" She slowly curled her fingers into a fist. Then she stalked off to the far end of the playground.

I gulped. I got the message real fast. No brownie, no life.

"She's really scary," whispered Claire. "What are you going to do?" A worried frown creased her forehead.

"I don't know," I answered miserably. "But I'd better make sure I have a brownie tomorrow."

Chapter 3

After recess Ms. MacArthur announced a scavenger hunt. We had to hunt down different things about different kids in the class.

I stayed as far away from Bethany as I could. I already knew too much about her, and what I knew I didn't like. But I did learn some pretty interesting things about some other kids in my class. For instance, James's favorite food is sauerkraut, Monique has six brothers and sisters, and Nicholas spent his whole summer vacation living on a boat. Pretty cool. I also learned that Ms. MacArthur doesn't like snakes. In fact, she hates them. I think she used the words "terrified to death." I already knew that Claire's best friend was me, because I'm *her* best friend.

Then Ms. MacArthur said, "Everyone partner up. We're going to interview each other. Try to pick someone you don't know very well."

I looked over at Claire. That kind of ruled her out. I shrugged. Maybe I could interview Rachael or Matthew. They had moved to Bayfield at the end of second grade, and I didn't know very much about them. Just as I was trying to decide which one to pick, Ms. MacArthur zoomed in on me. "Oh, Lauren! Would you be partners with Bethany? It would be nice to get to know each other. After all, you will be working at the same table this year." She handed us each a question sheet.

I glanced over at Bethany. She seemed to be as happy about being partners as I was. A scowl spread over her face. I could picture a thundercloud over her head, with a big lightning bolt pointing at me. "Sure, Ms. MacArthur."

I asked the questions first.

"What's your favorite food?"

"That's easy. Spaghetti."

"How many people are in your family?"

Bethany smiled. "Three. Just me, my mom, and my dad."

Maybe this won't be so bad after all, I thought. She's giving me the answers. She's not being a bully. She's even being sort of nice.

That lasted until I read the last question. "What can you bring to class tomorrow that will surprise everyone *and* they'll learn something new about you?"

Bethany smirked. "My boa constrictor."

The color drained from my face. "A boa constrictor? You can't be serious. You just heard Ms. MacArthur say she's terrified of snakes."

"Exactly." Bethany smiled. "Exactly."

Chapter 4

"Good morning, class," began Ms. Mac-Arthur the next day. "I hope you all remembered to bring in something to share with the class — something that will surprise us and tell something about you."

I glanced over at Bethany. She grinned and held up a pillowcase and I was sure I saw something wiggling around inside it. Something big and long and the size of — yup — a boa constrictor.

"Who would like to go first?"

Claire knew about Bethany. She frantically waved her arm in the air.

"Claire?"

Claire walked to the front of the room. "Last winter I went to Florida," she began,

"and I swam with the dolphins." She held up a picture. She was petting a dolphin. A big grin was plastered on her face. That had been the highlight of her trip, I remembered. For weeks after she came back to Bayfield that's all she talked about.

After Claire, lots of the kids showed interesting stuff. But I couldn't concentrate. All I could think about was Ms. MacArthur's terrible fear of snakes and Bethany's "surprise." Then I heard the dreaded words:

"Bethany, what did you bring in today?"

My stomach clenched into a knot. I

thought I was going to be sick. I wanted to yell, "Watch out, Ms. MacArthur!" But everyone knows you can't tell on a bully. Your life would get even worse. Right now I had enough trouble with Bethany. I couldn't handle any more.

Bethany strolled to the front of the room. I held my breath. I could barely stand to watch as she slowly untied the bag. I glanced over at Ms. MacArthur. She had a big smile on her face. Boy, was *that* about to change!

Bethany reached inside. She looked at me and smiled an evil grin. She seemed to be saying, "What are you going to do about this, Lauren?"

Then Bethany pulled out a long, thick, green . . . pool noodle.

A pool noodle? What?!

"This summer," began Bethany, "my dad put a pool in our backyard." She paused. "Since I couldn't bring in the pool, I thought this noodle would be a good idea. It was so cool floating around on it."

Ms. MacArthur beamed. "That sounds like great fun, Bethany."

I stared at Bethany. She smirked at me. "Got ya," she seemed to be saying.

"What a mean trick," complained Claire after school. We were sitting on the back steps with our snack of oatmeal raisin cookies and milk.

"Hmm." I nodded with my mouth full. "I'm really glad I didn't say anything to Ms. MacArthur. I would have looked so stupid."

"Yeah," Claire answered glumly.

"And what am I going to do about recess? I can't keep bringing her a snack every day. What will *I* eat?"

"I'll share with you." She dunked her cookie into the milk. "Don't worry. We'll figure something out."

I smiled at Claire. That's why she's my best friend. She sticks by me, no matter what.

Chapter 5

It didn't take Bethany long to find me on the playground the next day. One minute Claire and I were playing four-square. The next minute she was looming over me. "So, what have you got for my recess, Shrimp?" she threatened.

I stared up at her. Then I looked down at my double-fudge chocolate brownie. It was still wrapped up.

"I'm waiting," she snarled, and she took a step closer.

I knew I didn't have a choice.

"Here," I said, handing over my snack.

Bethany shoved the entire brownie into her mouth in one bite. She started to walk away, stopped, and turned back to face me.

"Remember, Shrimp, there better be another one tomorrow. Or else." Bits of chocolate clung to her lips and icing covered her front teeth.

I nodded. I didn't trust my voice to speak. My belly felt sore.

Claire looked at me. I could tell she was scared, too. "You okay?" she asked.

"Yeah, but she is such a . . . such a . . . *jerk*! I hate her."

"I know," Claire agreed. "Let's go play someplace else." She passed me her bag of pretzels. "Have some."

Right after recess we had math and then gym. Our gym teacher is Mr. Kempton. He's kind of old but he is always smiling. Today he had put out scooters for us to use. I raced in and around the pylons trying to beat Aaron. But he's really fast.

"Can't catch me!" he hollered as he flew around a corner.

"Nope," I laughed as I slowed down for the turn. Out of the corner of my eye I watched Bethany on the other side of the gym. She was having trouble on the turns, too.

"That's it for today, gang!" yelled Mr.

Kempton. "Everybody get cleaned up for lunch."

The bathrooms are always really noisy when we wash up for lunch. And crowded. Jenn and I were the last ones at the sinks.

"That was fun today," she said.

"Yeah. I hope we use the scooters again tomorrow. I so want to beat Aaron." I lathered soap on my hands.

"He's fast," she laughed. "He zooms around like a rocket." She dried her hands on some paper towels. "See you in the cafeteria."

"See you," I said.

Jenn headed out the door. I was just ready to leave, and who walked in? Bethany. She stared right at me and headed for the sink next to mine. I watched as she pumped the soap. She kept pumping and pumping until she had a big pool of pink soap in her hand. Then she dipped her finger into it and began writing on the mirror.

L A U R

She was putting *my* name on the mirror. The principal was going to kill me, or at least give me a huge detention.

"Wh-what are you doing?" I asked.

"Wait and see, Shrimp."

I watched in horror as Bethany continued to write on the mirror.

L A U R E N   L O V E S

"Stop that!" I cried. "I'm going to . . . " But I didn't get a chance to finish my sentence. Bethany took one step toward me and stared down.

"Who's gonna make me? You?" And she laughed.

I looked up at her. I could see the little hairs inside her nose and two big frowning eyebrows.

I stood a little straighter. I hoped it made me seem bigger. Taller. But my heart was pounding. I had to say something. "I — I —" I stammered. "I'm going to get in tr-trouble."

"So what?" Bethany answered. And she

painted the last few letters on the mirror.

JAMES

I could feel my face turn red. *James? Lauren loves James?* I couldn't leave that on the mirror.

"Now, that better still be here by the end of the day," said Bethany, "or else." She curled her fingers one by one into a fist.

Just then the door opened and Ms. MacArthur walked in. "Let's go, girls. It's lunchtime. We're running a little late." Her voice trailed off as she noticed the message on the mirror. She glanced from Bethany to me. "Just exactly what is going on here? Lauren? Bethany?"

I looked over at Bethany. I wanted to say, "Now you've done it. Now we're both in trouble." But instead I didn't say anything.

"I'll see you two girls back in our classroom after lunch. We'll discuss this issue then. In the meantime, one of you wash off the mirror. *Now.*" It was the crankiest I'd ever heard Ms. MacArthur sound.

"Yes, Ms. MacArthur," I answered. I reached for a paper towel. Bethany just smirked and followed Ms. MacArthur to the cafeteria.

Chapter 6

After the soap-painting incident, I tried to avoid Bethany for a while. Sometimes it was easy. Sometimes it was hard. But no matter what, she found me at recess time and I always handed over my mom's double-fudge chocolate brownie.

"I'm tired of giving away my recess snack," I complained to Claire.

She nodded her head in understanding. We were sitting in the cafeteria having lunch. All the third graders sit together at the last table by the window. "I haven't had one of my mom's brownies for two weeks." I stole a glance at Bethany. She was sitting at the end of the table quietly eating her lunch. She had a big slice of pepperoni pizza. I love pepperoni pizza. But I only get to buy lunch once a week. The rest of the time I bring it from home. Today my mom had packed a good one — tuna fish sandwiches with the crusts cut off, tiny gherkin pickles, apple juice, and pieces of cut-up celery filled with peanut butter.

"Claire, what have you got?" I asked. She was busy spreading out her lunch on the table.

"A ham and cheese sandwich, carrot sticks, yogurt, and milk." She dug into the bottom of her bag. "And this." She waved a granola bar at me.

"Trade you a celery stick for some carrots," I said. "It's how you like it — with crunchy peanut butter."

Claire smiled. "Sure."

We laughed and talked all through lunch, just like we always do. And of course Claire had a riddle for me. She has one every day. I don't know where she finds them, but she does.

"Bet you haven't heard this one," she said. "Ready?"

I nodded.

"How do rabbits travel?"

"How do rabbits travel?" I repeated. "Hmm." I thought for a minute, but I never can guess Claire's jokes. "I give up. How do rabbits travel?"

"By hare plane!" laughed Claire.

I laughed. "Good one."

"Speaking of traveling, look who's heading our way," said Claire. She tipped her head toward the end of the table.

Sure enough, it was Bethany. She had leftover pizza crust for the compost and a juice bottle for the recycling bin.

"Hey, watch this," I whispered to Claire. I took my last celery stick and scooped off all the peanut butter with my finger. Then I began tearing open the little packets of salt and pepper. "Quick, help me," I whispered to Claire. She stared at me as if I were crazy but she pitched right in.

"What are we doing?" whispered Claire.

"Watch," I answered.

Quickly I poured all the salt and all the pepper on the celery. Then I smoothed the peanut butter back on top. Perfect, I thought. Nothing to see but peanut butter.

"Claire, watch this."

Bethany was making her way back from the bins.

"Hi, Bethany," I said, waving the celery stick.

Bethany stopped. Then she frowned. "Hi."

"I was just wondering" — I paused — "if you want this? I'm stuffed." I patted my stomach.

She looked surprised. "Sure. I guess."

She snatched the celery out of my hand, shoved it in her mouth and began chewing. Then she stopped. Her eyes widened and filled with tears. She opened her mouth. I knew she wanted to spit it out, but the lunch lady was standing right there. She gulped and swallowed. There were a few choking gasps and then "Ahh-ahh . . . *choo*!" Chewed-up chunks of celery flew through the air. Some of them landed on the table. Most of them landed on Bethany's shirt. Tiny green gobs were stuck everywhere.

"Gross!" yelled Monique.

"Quick, move!" yelled James. "Before she does it again!"

But the words were hardly out when, "Ahh-ahh-ahh . . . *CHOO*!" The rest of the celery and slimy peanut butter sprayed all over James's face. He looked at Bethany in

horror. Her face had turned gray. I was pretty sure she was going to throw up. But she turned and ran out of the cafeteria. It was the fastest I'd ever seen her move.

I laughed and high-fived Claire. Pretty cool.

* * *

For the rest of the afternoon, Bethany ran back and forth to the water fountain. She just couldn't drink enough. On her last trip she leaned over and whispered, "You know, Lauren, you're even dumber than you look. And that's pretty dumb. And guess what? You're going to pay. Big time."

Suddenly what I thought was very funny was very *un*funny. Bethany would get even. Probably not today. Maybe not tomorrow. But she would get even.

* * *

"What a dumb idea," I lamented to Claire after school that day. "Why did I have to do that?" I threw the baseball. It landed with a loud smack in the middle of Claire's glove.

She looked miserably at me. "I know." Then she laughed. "But you have to admit, it was pretty funny." She threw the ball back. Hard.

I grinned back at her. That's one of the reasons we're best friends. No matter what, Claire can always see the bright side of things. Even today — now that I was on the hit list of Bayfield's biggest bully.

"You're right." I smiled. "I was sure she was going to barf. And," I paused, "it looked like she had green snot all over her shirt."

Claire laughed. "It was gross."

"And who knows, maybe now she won't want to eat my snacks anymore," I said.

"Speaking of snacks," said Claire, "how about we go inside and make one of my famous milkshakes? Extra ice cream."

"Great. Maybe we can come up with a plan while we're at it. You know, a plan that keeps me from being killed by Bethany."

Chapter 7

I didn't want to go to school the next day. I just knew Bethany would be waiting for me. I figured she needed some time away from me to cool down. So I came up with Plan B.

"Mom," I moaned, "I think I'm going to throw up. I can't go to school today." I put on my saddest face.

My mom looked at me strangely. "You don't look sick, Lauren. Come here. Let me feel your forehead."

As soon as she said that, I knew I was out of luck.

"Hmm," Mom said, her hand resting on my brow. "No fever. I think you're okay to go to school."

She continued to look at me oddly. Oh

boy, I thought. I am in so much trouble.

But I shouldn't have worried. Bethany wasn't in school that day. Or the next. Or the day after that. It was like a little piece of heaven. I got to be partners with Aaron and not once during those days did my stomach clench into knots. We painted pictures of our summer vacation. I decided to show Mom, Dad, and me camping at Vissers Beach. There was a crackling fire and we were all roasting hot dogs.

But on Friday my luck changed. Big Bethany came back.

She practically plowed into the room. She nearly knocked down James in the process. Then she made a beeline straight for me. I swallowed. *Oh no,* I thought. *This is it.*

Bethany got real close to my face. I could feel her hot breath. Her eyes were narrowed little slits. "I'm not going to forget what you did, Shrimp. You're going to pay for it. Big time. After school. *Today.*"

I gulped. What would she do? Stick gum in my hair? Punch me in the ribs? Dump Jell-O down my underwear?

"Boys and girls," interrupted Ms. Mac-Arthur, "please line up. It's time for our class picture to be taken."

"Whew." I breathed a sigh of relief. Safe for now.

I squeezed past Bethany, hurrying to stand in line next to Claire. Suddenly I felt myself falling. One minute everything was perfectly fine. The next minute I was pitching backward. I felt something wet soak my front. I glanced down. *Paint*! Red paint was all over my new top — and on Picture Day! I couldn't believe it. How was I going to get my picture taken now? They always put me in the front row because I was short.

The paint spread slowly across my top. It reminded me of blood. My blood. The blood that Bethany was after. And then I heard her snicker.

"Oops, sorry, Lauren. I didn't see you coming. Honest," she insisted. She made an X over her chest. "Cross my heart and hope to die if I should ever tell a lie."

She did not look one bit sorry. I couldn't prove it, but I was sure she had spilled that paint on me on purpose. My face got red. My eyes started to water, but I would not give Bethany the satisfaction of seeing me cry.

"That's all right." I stuck what I hoped was a smile on my face. "I'll just put my top on backward for the picture."

That's just what I did. I made a quick trip to the bathroom and switched it around. The paint felt cold and clammy on my back. When the photographer was ready, I gave my best million-dollar smile. After the picture I sneaked a peek at Bethany in the back row. She was staring straight at me. She didn't look angry. She looked . . . puzzled.

Chapter 8

"Class," began Ms. MacArthur when we returned from having our pictures taken, "we're going to start our very first project of the year. We're going to use the computers to research different states in America. Then you will present your information to the class."

She paused and looked around the room. "I'd really like to stress that the presentations need to be *cre–a–tive*." She drew the word "creative" out slowly.

This, I was good at. I've been using computers since I was four years old. I could find my way around on the Internet, use search engines, and do all sorts of other stuff. This was my kind of project.

"And you'll have a partner," added Ms. MacArthur.

I glanced over at Claire. I pointed to her and then back to me. She nodded and gave the thumbs-up signal. What a great team we were going to make.

"We'll draw names to see who you will work with."

The entire class groaned.

"Can't we pick our own partner?" whined Nicholas.

Ms. MacArthur smiled. "Maybe next time, Nicholas. This will be a good way to get to know someone new in the class."

She began to circulate around the room, handing out little slips of paper for everyone to put their names on. I wrote *Lauren Campbell* in my best writing, folded it my secret way, and dropped it into the basket. I crossed my fingers on both hands for good luck and hid them under the table.

Ms. MacArthur began to pull names out of the basket. "Kris, your partner is . . . " She

paused as she pulled another folded slip out of the basket. " . . . Rachael. Matthew, you'll work with James. And Claire . . . "

I held my breath. Please, please let it be me, I prayed.

"Your partner is Kirsten."

I groaned. I so wanted to work with

Claire. Now it didn't matter who I worked with.

"Bethany, your partner is . . . "

Oh no! Bethany! Of course it mattered. I could end up with the biggest bully in the school as my partner. I held my breath and repeated silently: anybody but me, anybody but me.

And then through the noise in the classroom I heard, "Lauren. Bethany and Lauren will be partners."

I closed my eyes and slumped in my seat. How could a day get any worse? My top was ruined. Bethany had after-school plans for me. And now I had to work with her for the rest of the day. What I thought was going to be my best year in school was rapidly turning into my worst year.

Chapter 9

Bethany shot a sly smile at me. "So, Shrimp, it's you and me."

"I guess," I answered, not meeting her eye.

"Well, too bad for you, I hate doing projects. So you can do it. All of it." Bethany crossed her arms over her chest. "This will be the beginning of payback time."

I gulped. "Well, I'm pretty good at using the computer. Why don't you pick a few places and I'll show you how to use a search engine."

"I already told you," Bethany raised her voice, "*you're* doing the project and *we'll* get the credit."

"Girls," interrupted Ms. MacArthur, "is

there a problem here? Bethany, you need to use your inside voice."

"No problem," mumbled Bethany.

"Have you chosen a state yet?" She looked at me and then at Bethany.

"Uh— " I stammered.

"Alaska," blurted Bethany.

"Really? That sounds fascinating." Ms. MacArthur wrote "Alaska" down on her clipboard.

I stared at Bethany. Alaska? Where did that come from?

"Well, I look forward to your presentation, girls." And with that, Ms. MacArthur was gone.

"How could you pick Alaska?" I cried. "*We* didn't choose it. *We* didn't decide on it. *We* didn't even talk about it."

"So, too bad, Shrimp. I used to live there. And one of us had to be quick on our feet and think of an answer. Duh. It sure wasn't you."

I inhaled slowly and deeply. There was no way this was going to work. I was not going to do the whole thing myself. And "Shrimp." Maybe I was short, but I was sick and tired of Bethany calling me Shrimp.

"Don't call me Shrimp anymore. I don't like it."

Bethany's eyebrows shot up. She looked surprised. After a moment she said, "Okay." She leaned closer. "Well, then, Computer Whiz, let's see you work your computer magic. Find some information on Alaska."

Just like that, Bethany had agreed to stop calling me Shrimp. I think she was as surprised as I was. We were off to a rocky start, but at least it was a start.

Chapter 10

We spent the rest of that day researching Alaska. Or should I say, *I* spent the rest of that day researching Alaska. Bethany spent the rest of the day staring at the computer. Her jaw was thrust forward. Her hands were tightly clasped on her lap. She looked meaner by the minute. Great. As if I didn't have enough problems on my plate.

It turned out Bethany knew next to nothing about computers. Not how to turn them on. Not how to use a mouse. Definitely not how to access the Internet. Every

time I showed her how to do something, she growled at me. Her face got redder and redder. Beads of sweat dotted her upper lip. She crossed her arms over her chest.

Great. Just great, I thought. Another reason for her to get even after school.

"Hey," I asked, "did you know that Alaska is known as the Great Land? And sometimes it's called the Land of the Midnight Sun?"

"Duh."

"It says here that in the summer they have twenty-four hours of daylight. That would be weird."

"Duh. Everybody knows that."

"Well, I didn't," I retorted. "Imagine being able to ride your bike in the middle of the night. Like it was daytime."

Bethany looked down at her lap, silent.

"And there's this thing called ar— aror— "

"Aurora borealis."

"Right! How did you know that?"

"That's the northern lights. They're bands of colors — green and blue and pink and yellow — flashing through the sky at night."

"Did you ever see them?"

"Sure," replied Bethany, "lots of times."

"Cool."

At that moment the bell rang. Time to go home.

Bethany glanced over at me. "I'll see you out at the bike racks, Miss Computer Whiz. Be there."

At least she wasn't calling me Shrimp any more. Computer Whiz was a bit better. I think.

But she hadn't forgotten. It was payback time for Bethany. I had been hoping that maybe, just maybe, she would let the celery incident slide by. Especially now since we were partners. Wrong. She was every bit as big a bully as kids said.

I dragged myself to the door. As slowly as possible I packed my lunchbox in my book-bag. Stall for time, I thought. Then at the last moment, head straight for the bus and sit right behind the driver.

"Hurry up, Lauren. You'll miss the bus," warned Ms. MacArthur. She sounded impatient.

"Okay."

I made my way down the hallway. So far so good. The coast was clear. No sign of Bethany. I pushed open the front door and shot a glance at the bike racks. Sure enough, she was there, bothering some second grade kids. I had a chance. Then she turned and saw me.

Caught!

It was now or never. I made a mad dash for the bus. I flew up the steps and into the seat.

Dennis, the driver, asked, "Anxious to get home today, Lauren?"

"Sure am," I panted.

Through the window I saw Bethany storming toward the bus. Coming after me. Her face was a dark thundercloud. Surely she wouldn't try anything in front of the driver. Just then a police car pulled into the bus loop. The window rolled down and the officer hollered, "Hey, Bethany! Over here!"

Bethany turned around. I could tell she was surprised.

This was my lucky day. Bethany was going to jail! Well, probably not jail. Maybe reform school, where bad kids go. The cops probably knew she was a bully, always making trouble for everybody else. They were going to take care of her, once and for all. Bethany was going to do time! I breathed a sigh of relief. No more Bethany.

I watched as she approached the police cruiser. And then I couldn't believe my eyes. Bethany smiled the biggest smile I had ever seen! She opened the door and hopped into the front seat. It was like she was happy to see the police. Weird. I'd be scared to death knowing I was going to reform school. But not Bethany. She's just that tough. She even smiled as she was being taken away.

And then it dawned on me. I no longer had a bully problem. With Bethany in reform school, third grade just got a whole lot better.

Chapter 11

Was I in for a surprise on Monday. There was Bethany sitting at the computer table. Just waiting. Waiting for me. So much for her being behind bars.

"I thought you went to jail," I stammered as soon as I saw her.

"What?" asked Bethany.

"I mean reform school," I said. "I saw the cops come and get you on Friday."

Bethany tipped her head back and laughed. I could see two fillings in her top molars. She was laughing that hard.

"That's the funniest thing I ever heard," she replied. "That was my dad who picked me up. He's a state trooper." She paused. "Why would I be going to reform school?"

I looked down at my sneakers. Gee, how dumb could I get? Now what could I say? So, I said the truth. I looked Bethany straight in the eye.

"Because you're always bullying kids."

Bethany stared back at me. Hard. Her eyes narrowed. But before she had chance to say anything and before I ran out of courage, I continued. "You took some little first grade kid's lunch money. You put gum on Rachael's seat and she ruined her brand-new pants. You threw a big rock through the gym window. And," my voice started to get louder, "you keep taking my recess snack! That's why you don't have any friends. Bethany, you are just plain mean!"

I closed my mouth. My heart was pounding. I was breathing so hard I thought I might faint. I couldn't believe I said those things. They were true, or at least I thought they

were true. But I shouldn't have said them.
I was dead meat.

Then the weirdest thing happened.
Bethany got this funny look on her face. For
a minute I thought she might cry. A red flush
started creeping up her neck. It covered her
face until even her ears were bright red. She
just sat there on her chair, blinking. Then

she said, "We need to get to work on our state project."

Just like that! As if I hadn't said a word about her being a bully. As if she hadn't heard a thing. But I knew she had. She just totally ignored everything I said. As if it never happened.

My heartbeat slowed down. My breathing returned to normal. I couldn't believe my good luck. "Oka-a-ay," I answered slowly. And for the first time, Bethany actually helped me with the project. Sort of.

I learned that Bethany had lived in Fairbanks for two years. On account of her dad's job. In fact, she's lived in three different places in Alaska — Fairbanks, Palmer, and Fort Yukon. She was like an Alaska Expert. Who would have thought that? Not me, that's for sure.

Later that morning during math, Claire met me at the pencil sharpener. "Are you crazy, talking to Bethany like that?" she whispered. "Everyone in the class heard what you said."

"I just couldn't take it anymore," I whispered back. "I'm tired of being bullied. Tired of hearing about other kids being bullied. And you know what?"

"What?" asked Claire.

"She was okay to work with after that. I mean, she wasn't super-friendly or anything, but at least she helped with the project."

"Hmm. Interesting," replied Claire.

Chapter 12

On Tuesday Ms. MacArthur announced, "Class, I'd like you to finish your projects by the end of the day. We'll start presenting them tomorrow." She paused, "And remember, I'd like you to present your state in an *interesting* way. You'll have this afternoon to work on the computers."

One more afternoon to work with Bethany. Then it would be done. And I, Lauren Campbell, would have survived working with Bayfield's biggest bully.

I glanced over at Bethany. Somehow things had improved since I told her what everyone thought of her. She didn't take my brownie at recess. She didn't try to trip me. She didn't wave her fist like she was going to beat me up. She was just there. I couldn't figure it out. But that was okay. As long as things kept on like this, I'd be happy.

We finished the computer work in the first twenty minutes and wrote two more facts on our chart. Then we spent the next little while making a poster. We drew pictures of a polar bear, a ptarmigan, and some other wild animals in Alaska. I did most of the drawing. Bethany did the coloring. I painted the northern lights. Bethany added sparkles to make it look like they were glittering. We finished with ten minutes to spare.

Now we had to decide how to present our work to the class.

"How about I explain about the northern lights and you talk about hunting for caribou?" I suggested.

"Maybe."

"Or I can point to the poster and you can read the stuff we found on the Internet?"

"Maybe."

"We could hold the poster *and* the chart

and point to the stuff we talk about . . . "

"Maybe."

"What is it with you and all these 'maybes'?" I said. I knew I sounded cranky. But I didn't care. Every time I suggested an idea, all I got was "maybe." Maybe, maybe, maybe.

"Duh," said Bethany. "Ms. MacArthur said present our project in a creative way. What's creative about *your* ideas? I'll tell you. Nothing!"

"If you can do better, go ahead!" I sulked.

"I think I will. Leave the presenting to me, Miss Computer Whiz."

I stared at Bethany. Leave the presenting to her? I don't think so. If it was anything like the computer work, she would just sit there and we'd get a zero.

The bell rang. Bus time.

Tomorrow we would present our project. Ready or not. We had lots of good information. Our poster was neatly drawn and colored. One of us could talk about Alaska, the other could point to the chart. That's how it was going to work. Fat chance Bethany would think of anything else.

Chapter 13

On Wednesday morning I had butterflies in my stomach. It felt like they were all doing some weird kind of butterfly dance. I hoped Bethany and I didn't have to present our project first.

We listened to Monique and Jenn's project on Hawaii. Then we heard Kirsten and Claire's project on Maine. Matthew and James went next. And the weird thing was, everybody did the same thing. They all read from their charts and pointed to their pictures. It was boring with a capital B.

I snuck a peek at Bethany. She was picking lint off her shirt. She glanced over at me and smirked. She seemed to be saying, "See, I told you your idea was dumb. Duh."

I started feeling even more nervous. Ms. MacArthur was expecting something interesting. Creative. My idea was just like everyone else's. Boring.

I wish I had paid more attention to Bethany, I thought. Too late now.

I looked around the room at all the uninterested kids. Some were yawning. Others had a glazed look in their eyes.

I figured by the time we were finished, half the class would be asleep.

Ms. MacArthur's voice interrupted my thoughts.

"Now for our last project today, we'll hear from Bethany and Lauren. The rest of you will have a chance to present tomorrow."

Slowly I got out of my seat. I clutched the poster to my chest. As I was heading to the front of the room, Bethany grabbed my arm.

"Listen, you read. Leave the rest to me."

She was dragging a large bag behind her. Larger than the pillowcase she had used to carry her boa constrictor–pool noodle.

I nodded. What have I got to lose, I thought? Anything would be better than more reading and pointing. And more bored-looking faces.

"Okay," I said. I glanced at the bag. Bethany was facing the blackboard. She wasn't even looking at the class. Great. Some presentation this was going to be.

"Stop looking at me," hissed Bethany. "Start reading."

"But shouldn't you be facing the front?"

"Read!"

I cleared my throat. "We did our project on Alaska." I glanced over at Bethany. She was digging into the sack. "It is America's most northern state. There are many native tribes in Alaska. Each one has its own customs. In the winter, people need to dress very warmly because the temperature can drop to negative sixty degrees."

The class oohed. Strange. I didn't think it was that exciting.

Then I saw Monique point to something behind me. I looked over my shoulder. There was Bethany pulling a long fur coat trimmed with red and yellow beads over her head.

What? A caribou-skin coat?

I continued reading. "Many people wear mukluks to keep their feet warm."

Out of the corner of my eye, I saw

Bethany digging around in the bag again. And sure enough, she pulled out two seal-skin boots. Once she had these on her feet, she reached inside the sack for a small, round drum. She began to softly tap the drum.

I stared. I couldn't believe it! What else did she drag to school? Now we had everyone's attention. No yawners. No one looking out the window. Even Ms. MacArthur sat up a little bit straighter.

I continued to read the poster. "A long

time ago, some of the Native people living in Fort Yukon used to speak Gwich'in. Today many of them are learning to speak this language all over again." The drumming stopped.

Clunk. Clunk, clunk.

Now what was she doing? I glanced over but I couldn't figure it out. She began pulling rocks out of the bag. Rocks? What was Bethany thinking? This had nothing to do with our project. Suddenly that good feeling disappeared. I could just see our mark going down the drain. She'd better not plan on throwing them. I could picture the two of us in for a whole month of detention. I swallowed and continued reading.

"The Iditarod is the famous dogsled race that takes place every March."

Clunk, clunk. Clunk.

I snuck another peek over at Bethany. She was still dragging out rocks. "Alaska really is a northern adventure." I kept reading.

"And," I said, "that wraps up our project on Alaska."

I closed my eyes and swallowed. Please, please, *please* don't throw those rocks. It would be just like her. Once a bully, always a bully.

Ms. MacArthur stood and began to clap. "Wonderful project, Bethany and Lauren."

I glanced nervously at Bethany. My eyes zoomed in on the pile of rocks. I couldn't believe it. I rubbed my eyes. Impossible. But it was standing right there. While I had finished reading our information, Bethany had built an inuksuk. Right there. At the front of the room.

It stood as high as Bethany's waist. Two arms stuck straight out, pointing the way to travellers.

Bethany smiled. This time it was a real smile. "*Mahsi cho*," she said.

Ms. MacArthur looked puzzled. "Pardon me? 'Mahsi cho'?"

"It means 'thank you' in Gwich'in."

Bethany high-fived me. "We did it, Shrimp — I mean Miss Computer Whiz — I mean — Lauren."

"No, *you* did it." I smiled. Probably my first real smile ever for Bethany. "Why didn't you tell me you were going to bring in all this stuff? You made me worry for nothing."

"What?" she answered. "I couldn't let you off the hook that easily. Not after that," she paused, " . . . *delicious* celery."

I smiled sheepishly. "Truce?"

"Truce."

* * *

I can't say that Bethany and I were ever good friends after that. We didn't hang out at school together. Or go to the store or the park together. In fact, we really didn't do anything together.

But I did find out that a lot of the stories about Bethany were just that — stories. True, she really did give Kris Vaughan a wedgie and she wasn't the nicest kid at Bayfield Elementary. But after that day there were no more knuckle sandwiches. No more snack-grabbing. And I never made any more special celery sticks. We had reached an understanding. I understood her a little better. And maybe she understood me a little better. One thing was for sure — third grade did turn out to be my best year ever.